First published 2011 by Nosy Crow Ltd
This paperback edition first published 2013
The Crow's Nest, 10a Lant Street
London SE1 1QR
www.nosycrow.com

ISBN 978 0 85763 243 2

Nosy Crow and associated logos are trademarks and/or registered
trademarks of Nosy Crow Ltd
Text copyright © Nosy Crow 2011
Illustration copyright © Axel Scheffler 2011

The right of Axel Scheffler to be identified as the illustrator
of this work has been asserted.

A CIP catalogue record for this book is available from the British Library.

Printed in China

1 3 5 7 9 8 6 4 2

P osy

www.worldofpipandposy.com

Pip and Posy

The Scary Monster

Axel Scheffler

nosy crow

It was a rainy day and Posy was a little bit bored.

She decided to do some cooking.

In the kitchen, Posy put on her apron and washed her hands.

First, she took out

the sugar

the butter

the flour and the eggs.

Then she stirred everything together.

She plopped the mixture into the paper cases.

Then she put the tin into the oven.

Careful, Posy.
It's hot!

Posy was waiting for the cakes
to bake when she heard a tap
at the window.

It was a big, **furry** hand!

Posy felt a little bit scared.
Whose hand was it?

Next, there was a knock on the door!

"Grrr!" said a voice.

Posy was very scared indeed.

The door opened. It was a monster!
"RAAAAA!" said the monster.

Posy started to cry.

Oh dear!

The monster came right
into the house.

But then Posy looked at the monster's feet.
She stopped crying.

"Hello, Pip,"
she said.

"Hello, Posy," said Pip.
"I'm sorry if I scared you.

Would *you* like to be
a monster now?"

Posy put on the costume.

"Raaa!" said Posy.
Pip laughed.

Pip and Posy went out into the garden

and played until tea-time.

Then they had a glass of milk,
and lots of cakes!

Hooray!